Painting Angels

by

Melinda Johnson

ANCIENT FAITH PUBLISHING

Chesterton, Indiana

Painting Angels
Text copyright © 2020 Melinda Johnson
Cover and interior illustrations by Clare Freeman

Published by:
    Ancient Faith Publishing
    A division of Ancient Faith Ministries
    PO Box 748
    Chesterton IN 46304

store.ancientfaith.com

ISBN: 978-1-944967-72-7
Library of Congress Control Number: 2020938383

We are grateful to the nuns at Holy Transfiguration Monastery in Ellwood City,
PA, for their helpful review of the depiction of monastic life in this fictional
monastery.

For Majesta, always,

and for every wise and loving person

who teaches me "the biggest rule of all."—MJ

CHAPTER 1

"SAM'S GOING TO BE at the monastery most days this summer, just like you," said Macrina's mother. Macrina and her parents were walking to church along the shady lane that wandered from their house in town through fields and orchards to the gates of St. Gerasim's Monastery.

Macrina stopped walking in the middle of the pavement. "Sam is coming to the monastery?"

Her mother nodded over her shoulder. "Move along, love, we're in the road."

"Will he be there every day? Not just Sunday?"

"That's the general idea. Sister Katherine told me last Sunday, and I forgot to tell you."

Macrina stalked across the road and stepped daintily into the grassy space under the trees. She stood still again. "But why? Why does he have to be there?"

Her father followed her and put an arm around Macrina's shoulders, gently urging her toward the monastery's open gate. "Keep walking, honey. We want to be there when Liturgy starts."

"I am walking." Her feet crunched onto the gravel drive leading up to the gates. "When I was coming last summer, Sam wasn't there. He was only there on Sundays, or once in a while." Macrina's voice squeaked. Her head drooped.

"It's nothing to be upset about," said her mother. "You're both eleven years old, so I'm sure you'll find ways to make it work. You know the sisters have always looked out for Sam, ever since he started coming as a little boy."

"What do you mean?" Macrina felt surprised.

"Think about it, love. They let him take that corgi all over the monastery, even into church. Remember when Sister Katherine started putting the little rug out for them in the back of the sanctuary, so Sam could have Saucer with him during Liturgy? And Sister Anna lets Sam go in and out of Sunday school whenever he needs to. I bet Sam's family thinks it's good for him to be at the monastery."

Macrina sighed. Sam never had to follow the same rules as the other children. It had often bothered her. Why would the nuns deliberately break the rules for Sam? Macrina had always assumed that nuns liked rules as much as she did.

"Will he be there every single day?" she asked, returning to the main point.

"I don't know," said her mother. "His family lives just a few minutes from here, so I'd imagine he'll come often. Here, love." She whisked two silk scarves out of her purse. "Let's put these on."

Macrina was not distracted. She could tie on a headscarf and argue at the same time. "I want to go to the monastery by myself, like I did last summer!"

"You can, honey. Nobody said anything was going to change for you. You can go just like you planned. I'm sure the nuns will be happy to have you."

"But it won't be the same!"

"Life is what you make it, kiddo," said her father. "I'm sure you don't need the whole monastery to yourself, and Sam doesn't either."

Macrina paused. "That's true. Just because he's there doesn't mean he has to be where I am."

"That's not a very friendly attitude, is it?" Her mother smiled suddenly. "Who knows? Maybe you'll find something you could do together."

Macrina opened her mouth and then closed it. She wasn't going to argue the point, because arguing was wrong, especially arguing with your mother right before you walked into church. *I'll just watch where he goes and go somewhere else,* she thought, turning back momentarily to run her hand over the rough stone pillar that held up the monastery gate. *I won't have to be near him. But it will be annoying. Why does he have to be there at all?*

Macrina believed God organized every detail of her life, and thus everything happened on purpose. By that logic, God must want her to spend time with Sam. Or else, God thought she deserved to spend time with Sam. Macrina shuddered.

She always felt that God used the events of her life to reward or punish all her actions and choices. It was a secret belief, but it was powerful. Macrina tallied up her good behavior and her mistakes every day and wondered what God would do in response to them. When good things happened, she wondered which of her choices God was rewarding. When bad things happened, she hunted feverishly through her memory for a mistake God might be correcting.

Macrina had never told anyone about her views on God. She had started to explain them to her mother once, but her mother said, "Macrina, you make it sound like you're playing chess with God, and you're both trying to outmaneuver each other!"

Macrina thought about this for several seconds. "That's not what I mean, Mama."

"It's what you said, honey. Think about what you said. You make a move, and God does something to you in response. Does that sound like the God you hear about in Bible stories?"

"Yes, it does," Macrina answered eagerly.

"Give me one example!" said her mother, setting her spoon on the stove top and turning away from the soup to gaze at her daughter in concern.

"Pharaoh is an example. He didn't let the Israelites go, and what happened? Plagues! And how about the Noah story? Noah was good, so he got a boat. Everyone else was bad, so they got to drown. Or how about Moses? He got to see the Promised Land from the mountain because he tried hard, but he didn't get to cross over the river and actually *BE* in the Promised Land, because he made a mistake!"

Macrina paused for breath, but it was clear she had more examples ready. Her mother held up her hand.

"I hear you, and I'm glad you know all these Bible stories. And now I want you to tell me one example of your chess-game God from the New Testament."

Macrina looked puzzled. "Why?"

"Just tell me. Tell me one time when Jesus behaved like you think He does."

Macrina's mind went blank. She bit her lip. There must be one. She was eleven years old. That meant she'd been in Sunday school for six years. Somewhere in her brain, there must be at least one Bible story about Jesus she could remember right now that would prove her point.

Macrina's mother smiled, picked up her spoon, and went back to stirring her soup. "You think about that."

Macrina had spent the rest of the day racking her brain for an example. She almost got out her Bible but then decided she should be able to think of it without looking.

Think about mistakes people made, she told her-self. *Who made a big mistake? I know! Judas Iscariot! He betrayed Jesus. And what happened? Well, he killed him-self, but God didn't do that—Judas did. Who else?*

She thought about Peter denying he knew Jesus three times on the night Jesus was betrayed. And what happened? The cock crowed, Jesus looked at Peter, and Peter was so upset he went outside and cried. But then Jesus made him a leader over the Church after His Resur-rection, so that wasn't a good example either.

Macrina felt frustrated. She knew that if the Bible didn't agree with her view of God, there was something wrong with her view, and Macrina hated to be wrong. But she had been explaining her life by this system for so long that the idea of stopping made her feel panicky. If she wasn't earning or losing points from God, how would she know why anything happened? How could she tell if she'd done the right thing or the wrong thing?

Macrina followed her parents up the three stone steps, through the open door into church. She lit a candle, kissed the icons, and walked quietly to her usual place near the iconostasis, facing John the Forerunner. Macrina stared at John for several seconds. *Are you an example of my point? You were Jesus' cousin. You spent all that time telling people He was coming, and you preached and baptized and yelled at the Pharisees. And . . . your head got cut off.* NOT *an example.*

Macrina stretched her neck and resisted a strong temptation to crack her knuckles. She couldn't settle into the service. Her eyes wandered to the place where Grace and her family usually stood, the same spot where Macrina and her mom had led Grace's family the very first time they came to church at the monastery. Another family was standing in Grace's spot today.

Do other people stand in our spot when we aren't here? Macrina wondered. *Don't they know this is our spot?* She looked down at her feet, the floor under her feet, and the slice of air between her own face and the face of John the Forerunner on the iconostasis in front of her. It was her place on earth.

Macrina blinked and blinked again. She flicked her long dark braid over her shoulder and tried to focus. Everything felt odd, uneven, out of place. Even her red dress, smooth from the iron and just the right length, felt limp and sticky.

Macrina turned her head again. Near the door, on a small green square of carpet, sat Saucer the Corgi. His pointed ears moved, alertly, tracking the sounds of worship around him. Sometimes he would tip back his head and gaze up at Sam, who stood quietly beside him.

Sam.

Sam stood still. His eyes roamed slowly from face to face, person to person, icon to icon. Macrina thought he looked like he was studying the faces, watching for something, trying to figure something out. His eyes came to Macrina. Macrina turned her head quickly, feeling angry and silly.

She straightened her spine and stared hard at the curly vine carved around the top of the chanter's stand.

Her eyes wandered back to Sam. She noticed that he had a band-aid on his right arm, near his elbow, and one end of it was beginning to peel away from his skin. Macrina's fingers moved involuntarily. *He needs to press that on again, or it's going to fall off.*

Sam moved his arm, and the band-aid came loose. Saucer caught it as it drifted lightly past the end of his pointy nose. He held it in his mouth for a moment, looking mischievous, then seemed to recall that he was in church and dropped it on the carpet, pretending he hadn't noticed it was there.

Macrina couldn't get her mind off that band-aid. She could make out a scab on Sam's arm where it had been. There were always band-aids in her mother's purse. Macrina was shocked to realize she wanted to slip one out and take it over to Sam. *That would be the nice thing to do,* she thought. *Or would it? I'm just doing it because it bugs me that his dirty old band-aid fell off!*

Macrina's mind snapped back to God, who apparently thought it was a good idea for Sam to be at the monastery all summer. *What if I'm nice to Sam? That would be the holy thing to do, right? Everyone would like me to do that.*

For a moment, Macrina felt comforted. It was such a relief to have approval from those around her, and from herself. Maybe summer wouldn't be so bad. But the feeling faded. *Being nice doesn't count if you only do it to get what you want!*

Macrina tugged at her braid and twisted the end around her finger. Her mother glanced down at her.

"Are you okay, love?" she whispered.

Macrina breathed out so hard her nostrils flared. "Yes!" she hissed. "I'm fine!"

CHAPTER
2

SAM SLIPPED OUT the back door of the church just after he took communion. He followed a plan of his own design each Sunday. Each week, he redrew it like a map in his mind. The map led him into the church, to the square of green carpet. It led him up the smooth wooden aisle to the iconostasis to receive communion then looped back down the aisle and out the door. This was a good map. It kept him from pressing through a crowd of people at the end of the service. He held the door open as he reached it, and Saucer trotted through. Saucer always knew what Sam was going to do.

Sam ran down the church steps and started along the path to the animal farm. Saucer galloped beside him.

"I'm going to see you all the time this summer, Saucer." Sam jumped as high as he could. Saucer jumped too. They went back to running.

"All the time. I can come any day I want, and that means all the time."

Saucer barked joyfully.

There was only one path at the monastery. It began and ended at the church door, and it traveled to the door of every building and the entrance to every garden. Sometimes it seemed to wander or go around in circles, but as long as you stayed on the path, you would never be lost.

When Sam reached the animal farm, he climbed onto the fence and perched on the top rail. Saucer sat on his haunches, staring up at Sam. His black eyes sparkled. His pink tongue hung out of his mouth.

"Goofy dog," said Sam. "You look funny when your tongue hangs out."

Saucer snuffed and threw back his head.

"Are you thirsty?" Sam slid off the fence and opened the gate.

Squeeeeeek. Click. Sam loved the noisy gate. Every animal in the little farm rushed to the edge of its pen to welcome him.

"Baaa! Baaa! Buk-buk-buk! Arf! Quack! Quack! Quack! Hee-haw!" His eyes went affectionately down the line. He saw Aero the sheepdog with his best friend Butterscotch the chicken. He saw Mary and Martha, the bunnies, hopping in circles. The goats—Hop, Skip, Jump, Et Cetera, and So Forth—reared up against the fence, bleating and nudging each other in excitement. Bethle-hem the donkey was staring at the goats. At the far end, eight ducks of various sizes were busily following each other around a small pond.

Saucer raced up and down the path between the pens, checking on all his animal friends. His pink tongue hung out of his mouth even further. It was a warm day.

"Let's get you some water," said Sam. He stepped around the patrolling corgi and headed back to Saucer's red doghouse by the farm gate.

Just as he reached down for the metal water dish, Sam heard a voice.

"Your band-aid came off in church."

Sam straightened up. Macrina stood outside the farm in the grassy space across the path, fidgeting with her skirt. Sam looked down at his right arm.

"Yes, it did."

Macrina waited for a second. Sam waited, too.

"That's a pretty big cut," she said.

"It was." Sam touched it lightly with one finger. "You can see it's scabbing up now. Scabs form when the body begins to heal a break in the skin. There are platelets in your blood, and the platelets stick to each other to make a clot in the hole in your skin, to cover it up. It dries up, and that's how you have a scab."

Macrina blinked.

"Unless you're a hemophiliac," added Sam. "Then your blood won't make clots like that. So you're like a hose with a hole in it. You just keep leaking until you bleed to death."

There was a moment of silence.

"Would you like this band-aid?" asked Macrina, holding it out.

"It's okay," said Sam. "I'm not a hemophiliac."

"But you had a band-aid on when you came to church. Are you sure you don't want one?"

"I don't need one anymore."

Sam picked up Saucer's metal water dish and started toward the spigot, which was mounted on the barn beyond the duck pond, at the back of the little farm.

Macrina lingered, the unwanted band-aid pinched between her thumb and finger. She could still see the scab as Sam walked away.

Sam's mind had moved on from Macrina. He reached the barn and held Saucer's dish under the spigot. Sam liked the spigot's handle. It was hard metal, painted green, and it had ridges all around it. He liked to grasp it and feel his fingers fitting between the ridges. He knew his hand wouldn't slip when he turned on the water. *When I grow up,* thought Sam, *I'm going to invent something like this spigot. It's going to be something you need every day, and it will work perfectly.* He squeezed the handle and felt the metal edges biting into his fingers. His hand felt strong. His bones were like the spigot—hard and useful. They worked perfectly.

Sam carried the water dish back to Saucer's red doghouse by the gate. Saucer trotted beside him and waited, panting, while Sam set down the dish.

Sam watched Saucer lapping up the water. Whenever Saucer was concentrating on something, his ears pointed forward instead of up. Sam reached down to scratch the furry place on the back of Saucer's neck.

"What about the other animals?"

Sam's head jerked up. Macrina was still standing in the grass, holding that band-aid. He'd already told her he didn't need it. He didn't want her helping with the animals. Why was she still there?

"Are the other animals thirsty?" Macrina started across the path.

"You can go away," said Sam.

"What?" Macrina stopped on one foot. Her eyebrows arched up.

Saucer dropped back on his haunches and pawed Sam's foot. The goats bounced over to the corner of the fence closest to Macrina and stared at her, bleating and nudging each other.

Sam stared at the animals for a few seconds then

at Macrina. "You're making the goats jumpy. Nobody needs that band-aid. You should go away."

Macrina's face flushed. "I'm just trying to help."

"But you don't have to. I don't need help."

"You are so rude!"

"So, go away. Then you don't have to hear me be rude."

Macrina whirled around and stomped away across the grass.

Sam relaxed. He dropped down on the packed earth next to Saucer's doghouse. Saucer climbed into his lap.

"We escaped her again, Saucer," said Sam.

Saucer licked Sam's chin.

CHAPTER 3

"SISTER KATHERINE, what are we going to do with the children this summer?" asked Sister Anna, bustling into the bookstore office where Sister Katherine sat behind a desk making notes for the fall catalog.

Sister Katherine looked up smiling. She almost always smiled. God had made her face in a smiling shape. "You mean Sam and Macrina? They're an unlikely pair, aren't they?"

Sister Anna clasped her hands and nodded. "They don't like each other."

"I noticed." Sister Katherine chuckled.

Sister Anna frowned. "I want the children to feel this place is a sanctuary for them. We're lucky to be so close to a town that loves us."

"We are. We're a monastery in a village, in a time and place where there are almost no monasteries or villages." Sister Katherine sighed. "Being stuck with your archenemy all summer isn't most people's idea of a sanctuary, Sister Anna."

Sister Anna clasped and unclasped her hands, as if she were kneading a tiny loaf of bread between her palms. It was a sure sign that she was worried.

"So, are Sam and Macrina expecting to have summer jobs here?" asked Sister Katherine.

Sister Anna shook her head. "I talked to both sets of parents, although not at the same time. They're hoping we'll let the children come often to do little chores around the place, with plenty of time to wander and pray and day-dream. They both need a chance to just *be*."

Sister Katherine set down her pen. "Do you know what I think?"

"Yes!" Sister Anna was so short that when she nodded her head, her whole self bobbed up and down. "Yes, you think it happened for a reason."

Sister Katherine's smile widened. "I do." She leaned back. "You teach them every Sunday. What do you think we can do to help?"

Sister Anna clasped and unclasped her hands again. "Should we do anything? Maybe we should just let God do whatever He wants."

Sister Katherine chuckled. "God will do whatever

He wants anyway. I'm just suggesting that we could be part of the plan."

"But what part?" Sister Anna frowned.

"Damage control?" suggested Sister Katherine.

"They're going to fight and argue all summer, aren't they?" Sister Anna's shoulders drooped.

"It's because they have nothing in common," mused Sister Katherine. "Maybe they'd get along better if we could find them a project that took up all of their attention and gave them common ground."

Sister Anna shook her head. "I don't disagree about the project, but you're wrong about the children."

"How am I wrong?"

"Sam and Macrina have a lot in common."

"Sam and Macrina?" Sister Katherine was startled.

"Oh yes," said Sister Anna, nodding and bobbing. "They're very much alike. They show it in different ways, but they both have to work out some inner tangles to get through the day, every day."

"That must be tiring." Sister Katherine looked thoughtful.

"They're each so busy with their own tangle that they don't realize the other is struggling too." Sister Anna smiled. "I think there's a good chance they'd understand each other better than anyone else does if they gave themselves a chance."

The sisters were quiet for a few minutes. Outside the open window, Sister Anna heard birds chirping and the soft sound of a summer breeze rustling green leaves.

"What could they work on?" asked Sister Katherine, returning to the conversation.

"Do we have anything that needs painting?" asked Sister Anna. "Most children love to paint things."

"I have a list of what we painted last fall." Sister Katherine opened a desk drawer and brought out a three-ring binder covered in blue denim. She flipped it open and ran her finger along the divider tabs, choosing a green one and turning to it. She read the first few lines of a list and looked up to find Sister Anna staring at the binder. "What?" asked Sister Katherine.

"I love lists," sighed Sister Anna. "One day, I will have lists of my own."

"You love children," replied Sister Katherine. "That's why you have a class of your own." She looked back at the list. "What about Saucer's doghouse and the other little huts in the animal farm?"

"I don't know about that. I don't think Sam would like Macrina to touch Saucer's doghouse."

"Good point," said Sister Katherine, closing her book. "But she could paint something else. The bunny hutch could use it, and so could Butterscotch's henhouse."

"That would take cooperation and planning," said Sister Anna. "And they would have to talk over who was going to paint what, or they would only fight."

"And that's why it's the perfect job for them." Sister Katherine smiled. "They're going to fight anyway."

"Well," said Sister Anna, taking a big breath, "this summer will certainly be interesting!"

SAM LOOKED LIKE SOMEONE had just asked him to eat live worms. *Good,* thought Macrina. *He'll leave as soon as the nuns are gone and let me do the job by myself.*

Sister Katherine smiled at the two children, who were standing in front of her desk in the bookstore office. "I'd like Macrina to start working on the bunny hutch, and Sam, you can work on Saucer's doghouse. I'll show you where we keep the cleaning and painting tools in the barn. You'll need to clean first, before you paint, so that you don't seal in any dirt under the new paint."

"Wouldn't the fresh paint cover up the dirt?" asked

Macrina, showing an intelligent interest in the task. Sam rolled his eyes.

"Well, dear, it would at first, but it would make the new paint bumpy, and it might crack after it dried. That's why we need to clean away the old paint and dirt before we put on a new coat." Sister Katherine chuckled to herself. "You can't put new wine in old wineskins," she added mysteriously.

Sam turned to Macrina. "Don't touch Saucer's house. I take care of all of Saucer's things."

Macrina opened her mouth but could think of no response that was holy enough to say in front of a nun.

Sister Katherine stood up. "Come along, you two. Let's go find some scrub brushes and buckets."

Macrina stepped around Sam and skipped into the

hall, where she stopped politely to wait for Sister Katherine. In the office behind her, she heard a rustling sound as Sister Katherine came around the desk.

"Don't worry, Sam," said Sister Katherine quietly. "The doghouse is your job."

Macrina sniffed. Sam could have his old doghouse. She would be through painting the bunny hutch before Sam even got started, and then she'd be free to enjoy whichever garden was farthest away from Sam and his bad attitude.

Sister Katherine came out into the hall. Sam trailed behind her. Macrina thought he was going to turn around and run off, but then she heard a scrabbling noise, and Sam's face changed. He pushed past her and raced to open the outside door at the end of the hall.

Saucer the Corgi bounded through the door. He

reared up on his stumpy back legs and wrapped his front paws around Sam's leg, as if he were hugging it. His nose waved in the air, and he yowled in a funny, sing-song voice that was almost human. Sam laughed. He crouched on the floor and patted Saucer with both hands, ducking his head back and forth to escape Saucer's joyful tongue. Macrina was startled at the change in Sam's face. It was full of light.

"Can you hold the door for us, Sam?" asked Sister Katherine, smiling at the boy and the dog. Macrina stood primly beside her, waiting to go out.

"Sure!" Sam jumped up and pushed the door open again. Saucer bounced through it and ran in circles on the grass outside, waiting till everyone was through the door. As soon as Sam let it close behind them, Saucer raced off toward the animal farm with Sam at his heels.

"Do you like painting?" Sister Katherine asked Macrina as they walked along the path.

"Yes, I do. And I don't mind cleaning the hutch first. I didn't ask because I minded," Macrina explained.

"I know, dear."

Macrina sighed. "Good. But I have another question."

"What's that?"

"What shall I do with the bunnies while I'm cleaning their hutch?"

"Oh, they'll have plenty of room in their pen. The hutch is inside it, so as long as you keep their little gate closed, you won't have trouble. When you start painting, we might move them into a box in the office so they don't get into the paint. They might like to help us out at the bookstore!"

Macrina looked doubtful. "Won't they get away?"

Sister Katherine shook her head. "I don't think so. We'll make them a nice nest in a big box and keep it up on the table in the back. Martha will probably sleep, and Mary will enjoy rearranging everything in the box."

Macrina shook her head. "Their names are backwards! In the story, it was Mary who sat and listened and Martha who was busy."

Sister Katherine laughed. "But we didn't know how they would be when we named them. They were just babies!"

"What about Saucer? Will you need to put him somewhere else while Sam is working on his doghouse?"

"Don't you worry about Sam and Saucer, Macrina," said Sister Katherine. "I'll take care of them. Just be friendly when you can and focus on your own task."

"I will, Sister Katherine," Macrina assured her. But she felt certain that Sam needed more supervision than Sister Katherine realized.

—

CHAPTER 5

SAM SAT ON THE BACK STEPS of his house. Sitting there, he could rest his feet on the ground, but he liked to rest them on the bottom step instead. On the dusty ground was a rough, oblong mark. Sam had made the mark by scrabbling on the dirt with his fingers. It was just the sort of mark a dog might make if he decided to plop down in the dust for a rest. Sam propped his elbows on his knees with his chin on his hands and stared at the mark.

A breeze whisked around the corner of the house and lifted sweaty strands of hair from Sam's forehead. It was a hot day.

The door opened behind him. Sam didn't turn around. He knew his parents by the sounds of their footsteps. His father walked smoothly, rolling from heel to toe like a runner. His mother walked firmly, almost marching through her day.

"Hi, Sammy." His father stepped out onto the stoop behind Sam.

Sam hunched his shoulders. "Don't step on my ground. I made something on it."

"No worries, my man. I just came out for some air, then I'm going back to finish caulking tile in the bathroom."

Sam swiveled around and looked up at his father. "There's caulk on your shirt."

His dad grinned. "That's why I'm wearing this old shirt. Caulking is a messy job."

Sam sighed. "I'm going to paint at the monastery this summer."

"You don't sound happy about it."

"Well, I *was* happy about it."

"What happened?"

"*Macrina*."

Sam's father squatted down and leaned his back against the door jamb.

"Macrina again, huh. What did she do?"

"So far, she didn't do anything. But she will. She tried to help put water in Saucer's bowl." Sam clenched his fists and stretched out his arms. "She could go away. That would help."

"You can't know the future, buddy. Maybe if you have a project to do together, it won't be so bad."

"I don't want to find out. I don't want to find out if it will be so bad."

His father rested a hand on Sam's shoulder. Sam hunched his shoulders and clenched his fists, stretching out his arms as hard as he could.

"Let's make a plan," said Sam's father. "The summer is long. You could have a good time if you had a good plan."

"Saucer will be there," said Sam.

"That's right. Saucer will be there no matter what. What else?"

"It wouldn't be so bad if Macrina would just leave things alone, but she never does. She comes around when I don't want her, and she messes with things. I don't want her in the farm with the animals. I don't want her talking about Saucer." Sam shook his head hard, the way a swimmer does when he wants to clear water from his ears. "I wish I could draw a huge line around all the animal places in the monastery and that she had to stay outside the line."

"Saucer likes to run around with you. He won't want to stay inside a line."

"No, the line is for Macrina. She has to stay outside the line."

"But that means Saucer has to stay inside the line."

"No!" shouted Sam, standing up suddenly. "The line is for Macrina! She has to stay away from Saucer!"

Sam's father sat very still and waited quietly. Sam stood rigid, breathing loudly.

"Do you know the definition of a line in math?"

asked Sam harshly. "A line is infinite. It goes on forever in both directions. Not even Macrina can go around the end of it."

"That's true." His father's voice was deep and calm.

The breeze came again, and leaves rustled in the maple tree behind the house.

"I know," said Sam. "The line won't work because it has two sides. One side faces Macrina, but the other side faces Saucer."

"That's exactly right, Sam." His father smiled at Sam, but Sam was staring at the maple tree, watching the leaves. "So, what's another plan you could make?"

Sam sat down heavily on the step. He rested his feet on the ground, one on each side of the dog-shaped mark. "I don't know yet."

"There are, let's see—I think there are four days left of school. You have four days left to think about a plan."

"Macrina should go away. That would be the best plan."

"The plan has to be something you can do all by yourself. You don't know if Macrina will want to be part of the plan or not," his father pointed out.

"I don't want her in my plan. My plan is to get rid of her."

"Not quite, Sammy. You can't get rid of her. Your plan is to help yourself enjoy your summer with Saucer at the monastery, even if Macrina is there."

Sam said nothing.

"Saucer is there, remember?"

"Of course I remember. It's the only reason I'm still going." Sam made a deep, melancholy growling noise and wrapped his arms around his head.

"Come on inside," said his father, getting back up on his feet again. "Let's have a drink of water and a snack."

Sam didn't move.

"You can have your snack here or in the house. Which do you want?"

"In the tree. I want to have it in the tree."

"I'll pack it for you. Wait right here."

The door closed behind his father, and Sam opened his eyes. He stared at the dog-shaped mark on the ground.

CHAPTER

6

MACRINA STOOD on the best stepladder she had ever seen. It was shaped like an upside-down V, with four steps up one side. When it was open, there was a little shelf that unfolded across from the top step. She could stand on the second step and set everything she needed for scrubbing the bunny hutch on the top step and the shelf.

Macrina had dressed carefully. Her hair was braided and wrapped up into a bun, to be out of the way. She wore her old blue T-shirt and denim shorts and her red rubber boots. But even though she had chosen clothes that wouldn't be harmed if she splashed water or paint on them, Macrina was being careful not to splash any more than was necessary.

Sister Katherine had given her a bucket of warm, soapy water and a stiff bristle brush. The bristles were so stiff they were as good as sandpaper. Macrina had started the morning standing on the ground, scrubbing the legs of the bunny hutch and the little ramp Mary and Martha used to climb into their house.

Mary and Martha scampered into the corner of their pen as soon as Macrina heaved the soapy brush out of the bucket. Martha cuddled down and napped against the fence. Mary hopped back and forth in front of her sister, keeping a suspicious eye on Macrina and nibbling an occasional scrap of hay.

Macrina climbed onto the ladder, more because she wanted to than needed to, and scrubbed the walls and the roof. The brush made a rough, shushing sound as she pushed it back and forth. Dirty water streamed down the hutch into the hay-strewn earth below.

"You should have started at the top," said Sam, behind her.

Macrina's nostrils flared.

"Now the legs are all dirty again."

Macrina whirled on the step and almost fell off. "If I can't come near the doghouse, you can't come near the bunny hutch!"

"You don't own the bunnies."

"Well, you don't own the dog!"

"Yes, I do!"

"No, you don't!"

"Hello, Sam," called Sister Katherine from the gate of the animal farm. "How's the doghouse?"

"Better than the bunny hutch," hollered Sam, without turning around. "Because it doesn't have dirty legs from having Macrina wash it bottom up instead of top down."

"The doghouse doesn't even *have* legs!" cried Macrina, furiously. She turned on the step, clutching the bristle brush with both hands. "Sister Katherine, please ask Sam to leave me alone. I am not bothering him. I didn't even look at the doghouse when I came in. But now he's criticizing me about how I scrub the bunny hutch. It's not fair at all!"

"But she's doing it wrong!" shouted Sam. "Started at the bottom. Dirty water from the top runs down. Now you have to do it all over."

"Since when are *you* telling *me* how to do things the right way?" shrieked Macrina, losing her temper. "This is backwards! It's all backwards!"

"No, you're the one who's backwards! You're the one who did it upside down." Sam raced to the gate of the animal farm and grabbed the top rail with both hands. "The world turned upside down!" He turned back to Macrina, and his face was alert, interested. "Did you know that when the British came to surrender their weapons to the Americans at the end of the American Revolution, the British band played a song called 'The World Turned Upside Down'? They did it on purpose. It was an insult to the Americans."

Macrina teetered on her step, clutching her scrub brush, speechless with rage and confusion.

"It was an insult," repeated Sam, deciding from

her silence that Macrina didn't understand what he was explaining to her. "The song was a signal to tell the Americans that the only way the British could be losing was if the world had turned upside down."

"That's very interesting," said Sister Katherine, opening the gate. "Sam, I came to get you because Saucer is tired of sitting with me in the bookstore. Come and take him for me. I'm sure he's smart enough to stay out of your way."

"The American Revolution is the best!" roared Sam, ducking past Sister Katherine. "I'm going to get Saucer!"

Sam ran down the path as if a fire-breathing dragon were after him. The breeze lifted his hair, and although his clothes were rumpled and dirty, Sam himself was fast and strong.

Macrina stayed on the top step of her ladder,

squeezing the bristle brush and grinding her teeth in frustration. Sister Katherine came through the gate and closed it gently behind her.

"You know he's right," she said pleasantly. "It is best to start at the top so the dirty water running down doesn't undo your work."

Macrina's eyes filled with tears.

"But you're right, too. If he's unwilling to let you help him with his work, he can't expect you to welcome his advice about your work."

Macrina choked. "He won't even let me *look* at him. And he keeps thinking that dog belongs to him, which it doesn't."

"The dog's name is Saucer," said Sister Katherine. "Saucer does live here at the monastery, but we all know that Sam and Saucer love each other very much, and we think love is sacred."

"But I like people to follow the rules," cried Macrina. "Nuns follow rules all the time. When we come here, we're supposed to follow the rules. I *know* we are. My parents say it all the time. All the kids know it. So why can't Sam follow rules and be fair and know what belongs to him like the rest of us do?"

Sister Katherine smiled. "Macrina, we do follow rules here, but there's one rule we follow more than any other rule. Always. It's the biggest rule there is."

"The biggest rule there is?" Macrina's eyes widened. The very idea of a biggest rule made her feel better.

"The biggest rule," nodded Sister Katherine. "Do you know what it is?"

What could be the biggest rule ever and still have something to do with dogs and scrub brushes? Macrina thought for a minute.

"Is it in the Bible?" she asked.

"Yes, it is," said Sister Katherine, watching Macrina's face.

Macrina couldn't remember any dogs in the Bible. Her eyes fell on the bunnies. Martha was still asleep in the corner of the pen. Mary was biting bits of hay and throwing them into the air. "Is it about cleaning and doing housework?" she asked, thinking of Martha and her many cares.

Sister Katherine laughed. "You keep thinking about it, Macrina. Think and scrub and be patient with Sam. That might be the best way to discover the biggest rule of all."

Macrina's shoulders sagged. "I hate when I don't know what the rule is," she confided. "What if I'm breaking it and I don't even know?"

"The world is full of people who are breaking rules and don't even know." Sister Katherine sighed. "Lord have mercy."

They stood quietly for a moment, Macrina on her ladder and Sister Katherine at the gate.

"I guess I better get back to scrubbing," Macrina said at last.

"God bless the work!" said Sister Katherine, and she opened the gate and walked away singing down the path.

CHAPTER
7

"SISTER KATHERINE, what happened out there?" asked Sister Anna, bustling into the bookstore office. "Sam charged in here, hollering about dirty bunny hutch legs, and took Saucer away. I thought it would be all right. He obviously isn't scrubbing the doghouse right now, so Saucer won't be in his way."

"No, Saucer is not in his way. He and Macrina had an argument, so some quiet time with Saucer is just what he needs." Sister Katherine set down her pen, reflecting that quiet time was something she might not have until the summer ended.

"Oh dear," cried Sister Anna. "Arguing already? That didn't take long."

"It was funny in a way. Sam was correcting Macrina. That's what started the fight."

"Well!" Sister Anna threw her hands in the air. "I thought it would be the other way around for sure!"

"So did Macrina. She told Sam that it was backwards for him to be telling her how to do things the right way."

Sister Anna nodded. "Yes, she does like to follow the rules. She likes to help other people follow the rules, too."

"That's a kind way to put it," Sister Katherine said humorously.

"But you know, she's not all wrong. It is important

to do the right thing, and respect for rules is good." Sister Anna shook her head sadly. "It's just one of those virtues that most people don't appreciate."

"It's only a virtue if the rules you are following are good ones. I think she struggles so hard because she's always straining after the speck and ignoring the log."

Sister Anna clasped her hands. "Yes, but I also think she struggles because she worries."

Sister Katherine frowned. "What do you think she worries about?"

"I'm not sure," said Sister Anna, "but it seems to me that she wouldn't be so critical of everything if she wasn't afraid of something. Maybe she's just as critical with herself. We don't know what she says to herself."

"Most people think she's like that because she's

naturally bossy, I'm afraid. But you know her better than I do, and your idea is just as logical." Sister Katherine got up to open the window. The breeze ruffled her habit. Threads of birdsong drifted into the room.

"Do you think we should separate them?" asked Sister Anna. "Maybe we're setting them up to fail."

"Helping them lead each other into temptation?" Sister Katherine sighed. "It would certainly be more peaceful around here if they didn't see much of each other."

The breeze fluttered the papers on Sister Katherine's desk. Sister Katherine gathered the papers into a pile, but the breeze came again, ruffling the edges. Sister Anna clasped and unclasped her hands, kneading, worrying.

"There must be a reason why they're the only two children God gave us for the summer," said Sister Anna suddenly. "If we separate them, they won't have a chance to work out what that reason might be."

"And making things more peaceful for ourselves isn't a very worthy goal, when I think about it," added Sister Katherine.

"What's the worst that can happen?"

"I have no idea!" Sister Katherine burst out laughing, and Sister Anna joined in her laughter.

CHAPTER

8

SAM'S MOTHER DROVE HIM to the monastery the
next morning on her way to the grocery store. The monastery had a large, iron gate that opened inward. Unless
there was a feast or pilgrimage, the nuns kept one side
of the gate closed and left the other standing open. Even
with only one side open, it was wide enough to allow a car
to pass through.

Sam's mother drove through the gate into the
gravel parking lot. When Sam climbed out of the car, he
saw two things. First, he saw Macrina walking up the side-
walk across the street. He saw her pause and look both
ways. She looked each way for exactly five seconds. Sam

counted. Then she crossed the street, walking toward the monastery gate.

The second thing Sam saw was a rabbit.

The rabbit's fur was brown and white, soft, almost sleek, like a pet, not a wild rabbit. He was sitting on the gravel outside the gate, only a few feet away from the side that stood open. Sam's mother hadn't run over the rabbit, but if he hopped a little further, any other cars would hit him!

Sam took a few steps toward the gate. The rabbit balanced on his hind legs, peering through the bars. One furry paw waved slightly, and two pink ears waggled as he sniffed the air. Sam saw that Macrina was nearing the gate. Would she startle the rabbit and make it run away? Sam tried to think of a way to alert Macrina without startling the rabbit. It was a problem he couldn't solve fast enough.

But the rabbit didn't run away. He wavered, then balanced, still upright, waving his wiggly nose in the air. Macrina stopped about a foot away from the gate. She gasped.

The rabbit and Macrina gazed at each other—the rabbit with curiosity and Macrina with breathless adoration. Very slowly and carefully, she knelt on the gravel, wincing as the rocks pressed against her knees.

"Hello, bunny," she whispered.

The rabbit dropped onto his four paws and hopped trustfully to Macrina. She held out her fingers, and the rabbit sniffed them. His tiny pink tongue flicked out and kissed her fingers gently, curiously.

"Come inside with me, bunny," whispered Macrina. "You aren't safe out here. Come inside and meet some other bunnies."

The rabbit sat up on his haunches again, considering.

"Sam," called Macrina in a low, urgent voice. "Sam, can you hear me? We need to bring this bunny inside."

"I'm coming," began Sam, looking around for something to catch a rabbit in.

"Sammy, look," said his mother, who had gotten out of the car to see what Sam was staring at. "I don't have a box, but you could try catching him in this picnic blanket."

Sam took the blanket, holding it against his chest, and crossed the gravel to the open gate. The rabbit hopped a few steps along the grass away from the gate. Still crouching, Macrina scooted along beside him.

"Sam, go behind me so you can get in front of

him. Then you can block him with the blanket."

Sam tiptoed past Macrina and unfolded the blanket on the gravel in front of the bunny. The rabbit sniffed the edge of the blanket.

"If we had a carrot, he would hop right on," said Sam.

"Hop on the blanket, little bunny," coaxed Macrina. She leaned closer, making a circle with her arms like an opened hug. "This way, bunny. Onto the blanket."

The rabbit hopped onto the blanket.

"We have to move slow," said Sam, letting his hands inch along his side of the blanket.

"Very slow," agreed Macrina, never taking her eyes off the rabbit.

The rabbit hopped to the middle of the blanket. He sat up on his haunches again and began to wash his face with his front paws.

"This is the cutest thing I ever saw happen in my whole life," breathed Macrina.

"I think this rabbit should be in the monastery animal farm," whispered Sam.

"What if he belongs to someone?" Macrina looked as if she hoped he didn't.

"They don't deserve to have him if they can't keep him safe."

Sam and Macrina stared at the adorable bunny.

"Well," said Macrina, struggling to do the right thing, "we could keep him here at least until someone comes to find him."

"And maybe nobody will come," added Sam.

"We can call him Lazarus," Macrina decided. "He can have a hutch next to Mary and Martha."

"He's not their brother," objected Sam.

"Then he can be named for the other Lazarus," said Macrina, "the one who lay outside the rich man's gate, asking for food."

"Because we found him outside the monastery gate," Sam nodded.

They stared at each other, startled to be in such perfect agreement.

"Tell me when you're ready to lift," said Macrina.

"One. . . . two. . . . three. . . ." whispered Sam, and they lifted the corners of the blanket and stepped toward each other, making a hammock for the bunny.

The rabbit hopped once or twice in the hammock, but he seemed more pleased than nervous. He cuddled down in the center and let them carry him carefully through the gate into the monastery.

Sister Anna, coming along the path, called out to them. "What do you have in the blanket?"

"The cutest bunny in the world!" answered Macrina.

"He's coming to live at the monastery," announced Sam.

"Where did he come from?" asked Sister Anna, peering down into the blanket. "Oh, he is a sweet little bunny!"

"He was outside the gate, near the road," Macrina explained. "It's not safe for him there, so Sam brought this blanket from his car and Lazarus hopped right onto it. He wasn't scared of us at all!"

"What a perfect name for him!" Sister Anna clasped her hands together, smiling. "He lay outside our gate, and you have brought him in. This bunny is having a much better time than his namesake did!"

Sister Anna walked ahead, and Macrina and Sam followed her, still carrying the blanket like a hammock between them. Macrina peeped at Lazarus every few steps.

"Don't worry," Sam told her. "See how still he sits?"

"Maybe he's sitting still because he's terrified."

"No, he isn't terrified. He's relaxing."

"I hope you're right." Macrina sighed. "I'm going to hold him when we get to the animal farm."

Sam nodded. "You hold him, and I'll help Sister Anna get the other hutch out of the barn. She can't carry it by herself."

Sister Katherine watched the little procession as it passed outside her office window. She wondered what was in the blanket. "The Lord moves in mysterious ways," she murmured, crossing herself.

CHAPTER 9

As soon as Lazarus was tucked safely into his hutch, Sam and Macrina tiptoed into church for matins. Saucer tiptoed with them. Macrina's mind was so full of Lazarus the bunny that she floated peacefully through the service without once thinking about Sam.

After matins, the children walked to the refectory with the sisters and shared their breakfast. It was a good breakfast. Sam made himself a peanut butter sandwich. Macrina had oatmeal with maple syrup on it. The morning sun shone through the windows, making the world seem fresh and bright.

At the end of breakfast, the sisters rose and said a prayer, thanking God for the food just eaten. Then a gently murmuring stream of nuns flowed through the room, tidying up after breakfast and walking away to other parts of the monastery for daily work. Sister Katherine called Sam and Macrina over to where she waited near the door with Sister Anna.

"We need to find out if Lazarus belongs to someone," began Sister Katherine.

Macrina interrupted. "We know, we thought of it, but we can keep him while you ask people, can't we?"

"Yes, you can. Just remember that if we find he belongs to someone, he'll have to go home."

"I hope he doesn't," said Sam firmly.

"And if they didn't keep him safe, shouldn't we keep him anyhow?" asked Macrina.

Sister Anna shook her head. "Animals escape sometimes no matter how careful you are. We wouldn't want to take him away from someone who loved him."

"And he doesn't look like a wild rabbit," remarked Sister Katherine. "Although we have seen wild ones like him, over the years. It happens when some farmer's rabbits get loose and start living in the woods. Their children and grandchildren still look like they came from the farm."

"But right now we're going to keep Lazarus," Sam insisted.

"Until someone claims him, we are," agreed Sister Anna.

"Is it time to work?" asked Macrina, who didn't want to think about Lazarus going away.

"No scrubbing and painting today," Sister

Katherine decided. "This is a day to enjoy Lazarus the bunny while he's here."

Macrina's face relaxed into a grin. "I can't wait to hold him and pat him again! He feels so soft."

Sam frowned. "I need to introduce Lazarus to Saucer. Lazarus is part of the herd now. Saucer has to know."

"What do you mean?" asked Macrina. "Do you have to train him not to hurt the bunny?"

"No, I don't mean that at all."

Sam turned away from Macrina. He pushed the door open, walked through it, and let it shut behind him before Macrina could follow.

"He's mad again!" cried Macrina, before she could stop herself.

"No, not mad exactly." Sister Anna shook her head.

"Macrina, dear, how do you feel when you say something to one of your friends, and your friend has no idea what you meant?"

Macrina looked uncertain.

"Do you feel frustrated?"

"Well, I try to keep explaining," Macrina said. "The right thing to do is be patient and explain again until the other person knows what you meant." She stopped, realizing it sounded like she was telling a nun what to do. "I mean, is that the right thing?"

"That's one right thing," said Sister Anna. "But there's another right thing to do."

"There can't be more than one right thing." Macrina was worried. "One of them must be righter than the other right things."

"Why do you think that?" Sister Katherine was interested.

Macrina swallowed. Here she was again, faced with the chore of explaining to an adult about the system she had set up between herself and God.

"Please tell us," urged Sister Anna. "We'd like to know what you think."

Macrina folded her hands, just like Sister Anna was always doing. "Because," she began. "Because of God."

The sisters waited.

"Because God is in charge of everything, and He decides what to do based on whether you picked the right thing or the wrong thing," blurted Macrina. "Every day, you have to make the right choices so He will reward you.

You have to figure out what they are, and you can tell how you did by what happens. If good things happen, He's rewarding you for picking right. If bad things happen, that's what you get for making mistakes, and you have to figure out what the mistakes were so you can pick right the next time."

Macrina stopped for breath and stared up at the nuns. They looked sad. Macrina felt frightened. "Never mind," she gulped. "Can we just pretend I didn't say all that?"

Without waiting for an answer, Macrina slipped out the door and raced across the grass toward the animal farm.

Sam was sitting on the top rail of the fence by the gate of the animal farm. Saucer was sitting below him, gazing up at Sam's shoes, which were resting on the fence rail above him. Saucer sniffed at the shoes and nipped at the ends of Sam's shoelaces.

Macrina leaned on the gate, panting.

"Why did you run?" asked Sam.

"Let's play with Lazarus," Macrina said, opening the gate.

Squeeeeak . . . Sam smiled. He loved the sound of the squeaky gate and the voices of the animals that sang out after it. "Buk-buk-buk! Arf! Arf! Baaaaa! Quack quack quack!"

Macrina shut the gate neatly behind her. Sam dropped down off the fence, and they walked together the short distance to the bunny hutches. The hutches were in two pens—Mary and Martha together in the first pen with their hutch, and Lazarus in the pen next door, with a hutch that had been hauled out of the barn for him. "It needs washing," observed Macrina.

"Not today," replied Sam.

Macrina sighed. She suddenly felt very tired. "I'm going into this pen," she said. She found the latch, flipped it over, and pushed the wire gate open just wide enough that she could wriggle through it. "Hello, Lazarus the bunny!" Macrina crouched on the dusty ground. Lazarus watched her for a few seconds, munching a piece of grass. The grass waved and wagged as Lazarus chewed it, but it got shorter and shorter until it disappeared into his soft pink mouth. Macrina was enchanted.

Sam leaned down to pat Saucer then caught his collar and gently turned his head so that he was looking toward Macrina and Lazarus.

"That's your herd, Saucer," Sam told the corgi.

"That rabbit is Lazarus. You had two rabbits. Now you have three."

Saucer pressed his pointy nose through the wires of the little gate, snuffing loudly.

"Are you sure he doesn't want to eat Lazarus?" Macrina lifted the bunny and cuddled him against her neck. "Oh, he's so soft!" Her face flickered like candle-light—worried for a few seconds, blissful for a few seconds. "Oh, Lazarus, you are the sweetest ever!"

"Bring him closer," urged Sam.

"Why?" Macrina asked, worried again.

"To teach Saucer."

Macrina frowned.

"Trust me," said Sam. "I won't open the gate."

Macrina walked slowly forward.

"Can you bring him down lower? Saucer is short!"

She crouched inside the fence, and Saucer leaned towards her, pressing his eager face against the wires.

"See, Saucer? That's our rabbit. You protect him. Always."

Sam gave Saucer a pat and then, without speaking, he climbed over the little gate into the pen and sat down on the dirt. He sat very still. Saucer watched him. Macrina watched him, too. After a minute, she sat down next to him, still cuddling Lazarus, who was getting sleepy.

The summer breeze drifted around them, soft and dusty. The air smelt of animals and sometimes of sun-warmed apples ripening in the nearby orchard. Saucer flopped in the dust outside the pen. His front legs stretched out in front of him. His back legs stretched out behind him. Saucer rested his chin on his front paws and watched over his herd.

THREE DAYS LATER, after a weekend away at her grandmother's, Macrina returned to the monastery, climbed her ladder, and began scrubbing Butterscotch's henhouse from the top down. Her socks inside her red boots were not sliding down. Her painting shirt was neatly tucked into her denim shorts. Her braid was twisted into a tight bun. But she felt rumpled and irritated from the top of her head to the tip of her toes.

She tried to focus on Lazarus, basking in the hay a few feet away in the bunny pen, but she couldn't. With every stroke of the bristle brush, she was doing what Sam had said she should have done on the first day. She was living out the fact that Sam had caught her making a mistake, and she was here right this minute because Sister Katherine had asked her to try again.

"Try again," muttered Macrina to herself. "Try again, try again. Try again on scrubbing top-down. Try again on not being annoyed with Sam. Try again on guessing what the biggest rule of all is because Sister Katherine won't just tell me, so I have to guess for myself, and I hate that."

The gate squeaked behind her, and she knew without looking that Sam had arrived at the animal farm. She heard the soft sound of Saucer panting in the heat and the little thuds of their feet on the packed earth around the doghouse.

"Nobody came to take Lazarus home yet," said Sam.

"I know," said Macrina.

"I don't think anyone will come for him," said Sam, after a moment.

"Why not?" Macrina wiped sweat off her forehead.

"If someone lost their rabbit, they would be out looking for him. Nobody is."

"Not that we know of, anyhow."

"This isn't a big town. If they were looking, we would know."

Macrina realized Sam was probably right. She even hoped he was. But she couldn't open her mouth and say it.

Instead, she dunked her scrub brush in her bucket and reached across to scrub the other side of the henhouse roof. It was just big enough that she couldn't scrub it well from this side. She dropped the brush into the bucket, got down off her ladder, and moved everything to the other side of the henhouse. When she had climbed up and fished out her brush, she could see Sam and Saucer. Macrina gritted her teeth and went back to scrubbing.

Sam stood by the doghouse, resting his hands on the shingled roof. "You're doing it right this time," he said.

Macrina breathed through her nose three times loudly.

"You started at the top."

Macrina opened her mouth, but Sam suddenly turned his back on her and started wrestling with Saucer. Fine. She didn't have to answer.

Macrina finished the roof and came down one step on her ladder to start on the walls. Little streams of sweat trickled down her back. Strands of hair slipped from her bun and clung to her neck and forehead. "Pretend it's the fiery furnace," whispered Macrina to herself. "Pretend you're walking in the flames with the angel, and Nebuchadnezzar can't believe you aren't dead in here."

Sam stopped wrestling with Saucer and stood up. "Are you talking to yourself?"

"Many adults talk to themselves," Macrina answered primly.

Sam took a step closer. "I talk to myself."

Macrina closed her mouth tightly. She got some fresh water on her brush.

"I talk to myself," Sam repeated.

"You don't say the same things that I do," snapped Macrina.

"I don't want to say the same things that you say." Sam started pacing out a square shape on the path between the pens—four steps forward, four steps across, four steps backward, four steps across.

"Well, everyone's different," said Macrina, trying to feel gracious.

"You look cranky today," Sam remarked, pausing to peer up at her face.

"I didn't used to be this cranky!" wailed Macrina. "Can you just let me scrub by myself? Why don't you scrub the doghouse?"

"Because you're not my boss," said Sam, firmly.

"You're not *my* boss!" shouted Macrina. "Why

can't you follow the plan? If you just leave me alone, and I leave you alone, we can both do our jobs without getting in trouble!"

"I'm not in trouble! Nobody's in trouble!"

"Good!" Macrina was trying to get control of her voice, but she couldn't. Suddenly, all she could do was shout at the top of her lungs. "I don't want to be in trouble! I don't ever want to be in trouble! I want to pick all the right things! Why won't anybody around here let me pick the right things?" The scrub brush dropped out of her hands, and she sank down on the top step of the ladder and burst into tears.

"Nobody is doing anything to you," countered Sam, still carrying on the conversation.

Macrina started to speak, choked, and cried harder. Sam rubbed his ears. Macrina's cries were loud, rough sounds. Did it hurt her to cry like that? How could she breathe? Sam bent his head, trying to see her face, but her hands covered it. He took a step toward her and tapped her elbow with one finger.

"STOP!" shrieked Macrina. Her fingers scrabbled around her eyes, trying to wipe the tears that wouldn't stop coming.

Sam edged away, glancing over his shoulder toward the gate.

"Can you still breathe okay?" asked Sam loudly. "I'm just checking."

"Go awaaaaaay!" wailed Macrina, flinging her arms around her head and crying harder than ever.

"Help!" shouted Sam as loudly as he could. "Sister Katherine! Sister Anybody! HELP!!!"

Macrina wanted to stop crying before the nuns

came, but she couldn't. She couldn't see well enough to climb down her ladder. She felt like the whole world had gotten out of her control and was rolling away from her like a snowball going downhill. She rested her face on her lap and cried so hard she got hiccups.

"SAUCER COME WITH ME!" Sam's voice sounded like a radio with the volume button pushed all the way to the top and stuck there. "SAUCER, COME!"

Sam yanked the gate open and charged out of the animal farm. Saucer scampered after him, barking and yowling.

"Help! Help!" Across the grassy space outside the farm, Sam could see a tall nun and a short nun running out of the bookstore. "You better go get Macrina!" he yelled over his shoulder as he passed them. "She's too much for me!"

Sister Katherine poked her head back into the bookstore, calling loudly to someone inside to go to Macrina at the animal farm. Then she and Sister Anna hurried after Sam, who was running as fast as he could toward the parking lot, with Saucer galloping beside him.

Behind them, a small quiet figure stepped out of the bookstore, closed the door gently behind her, and began to walk across the grass, leaning on a beautifully carved wooden staff.

CHAPTER

11

SAM RAN THROUGH the monastery gate, down the shady lane, into a smaller lane, up his driveway, and onto the front porch, with a barking corgi and two panting nuns running after him all the way. All four arrived breathless and hot. Saucer's tongue hung out of his mouth, flapping like the tail of a kite.

Sam's mother flung the door open as Sam scrambled up the steps. His flailing arms knocked over a potted plant before he bumped into the porch swing and collapsed onto its blue gingham cushion.

"Sammy! What happened? Are you all right?"

"Too much screaming," croaked Sam. "Macrina is too much."

"Why did she scream?" asked his mother, stepping out onto the porch.

"Because I talked to her. That's all! Talking makes her scream." Sam swallowed. "I can't go back there. Saucer needs to live at my house now." He paused. "Also, I need water!"

"You all need water," exclaimed his mother. "Sister Katherine and Sister Anna, I'm so sorry. I'm so, so sorry! Let me get you all a cold drink, and then you can tell me what happened. Sammy, can you stay on the swing?"

Sam nodded wearily. Saucer tried to climb onto the porch swing, but his legs were too short and the swing was too wobbly. Sam hoisted him up, and Saucer lay down beside his friend on the cushion.

"You sit with him," said Sister Katherine to Sam's mother. "I'll get the drinks."

Sam's mother crouched down next to the swing. She didn't touch Sam, but her hands smoothed the cushion next to where his hands rested.

Sister Anna sank into a chair on the other side of the door from the porch swing. Finding a magazine on a small table beside her, she flapped it in front of her face like a fan.

Sam pushed the porch floor with his foot to start the swing moving, then he wrapped his arms around Saucer and closed his eyes. No one spoke.

The screen door opened again, and Sister Katherine backed out onto the porch, carrying a tray. Sam's mother stood up to help her.

Sam could hear the ice cubes tinkling against the glasses. He could smell the pungent sweetness of lemonade. But he was too worn out to open his eyes.

"Can you try again to tell me what happened?" asked Sam's mother.

Sam didn't answer. His mother turned to the nuns.

"We're not sure," said Sister Anna. "You were with us in the bookstore for a little while, weren't you, Sam? And then you went back to the animal farm with Saucer. Macrina was scrubbing the chicken house this morning. Did something happen with the animals?"

Sam spoke without opening his eyes. "Macrina got stuck."

"Is she okay?" asked Sister Katherine, starting to get up.

"Not that kind of stuck." Sam opened his eyes and looked at his mother. "STUCK."

His mother nodded and touched his hand lightly, with just one finger. She turned her head to Sister Katherine. "That means Macrina was angry or sad and couldn't calm down."

"Stuck," agreed Sam, closing his eyes again.

For a few minutes, the three women said nothing. Sam heard them sipping lemonade. He heard the creak of porch furniture and the whisper of a nun's habit moving in the warm breeze. His throat was hot and dry. He wanted some lemonade, and he wanted a break from people and their sounds and emotions. Sam sat up. "I'm going inside, Mom." He stood up slowly, moving toward the door. Saucer lifted his head from the cushion, raised himself on his short legs, and hopped down onto the porch, trotting after Sam into the house.

"I think Saucer should stay with him," Sister Katherine spoke into the silence.

"That's so kind. I'm so sorry. We'll talk to Sam tonight about not running off. He's usually good about that. I'm sorry for all the drama. I've been worrying we're asking too much of you this summer. Sam and Macrina have always struggled. . . ." Her voice caught in her throat. She swallowed. "I'll bring the dog back in just a little while."

"There's no rush," said Sister Katherine, soothing her. "You aren't asking too much. We wouldn't let the children come if we didn't want them."

Sam's mother sat down on the swing and looked up at the two nuns. "You have been so good to him. I can't even explain—the monastery—having somewhere to go where he's safe and feels love and can almost be independent." Her voice broke.

"He's good for us, too." Sister Katherine reached over and patted Sam's mother gently, blessing her. "Keep the dog here. God made them for each other. We won't stand in His way."

Sister Anna nodded. "He can come over every day, just like he does now, and Saucer can come with him. They can stay with us for whatever time they need, and then Saucer can come home with him at night."

"We'll keep his doghouse at the animal farm, because Sam and Saucer both love that. What about here? Could he sleep inside with Sam?" asked Sister Katherine.

Sam's mother nodded, clasping her hands over her heart. Tears ran down her cheeks into the tiny smile creases around her mouth. Her face shone with hope and love. She turned to gaze at the open door her son had walked through. "Oh, my Sammy," she whispered. "God truly holds you in His hands."

CHAPTER 12

"Why do you cry, Macrina?"

Without looking up, Macrina stuffed her fingers into the pockets of her shorts, seeking frantically for a tissue. A pack of tissues appeared in front of her, shaking slightly because Gerontissa was very old, and her hands trembled when she could not rest them on her cane.

Macrina cried harder.

Gerontissa came closer. Macrina could feel the abbess's soft, wrinkled hands cradling her fingers, guiding the tissue up to her tear-stained face.

"S-sorry . . . Th-thank you," wailed Macrina.

"Little one, you are very sad," murmured the kind old voice. "You love this place, no? You are never sad here, till now."

"It's ruined!" sobbed Macrina. "Because of Sam, but because of me. God ruined it because of m-meeee!"

Gertonissa let go of her hand and grasped her arm, gently but firmly. "You come from off this ladder. We will leave the chicken house."

Macrina stood up warily. Her eyes were blurry with tears, her nose was running, and she had a confused and frightening sense that she was in trouble with the abbess, the head nun of all the nuns, the one she had always thought must love the rules the most. Macrina took two wobbly steps down the stepladder.

"Yes, good." Gerontissa waved her cane in the direction of the gate. "Now, we go."

Gerontissa walked slowly because she was very old, and Macrina walked slowly because she was very sad. She discovered that she was still clutching a tissue in one hand, so she blew her nose.

"I have more tissue," Gerontissa remarked cheerfully. "You tell me if you need one."

"Yes, Gerontissa." Macrina hiccupped. "Yes, please."

Gerontissa stopped walking, let go of Macrina's arm, and reached into a deep pocket in her long black robe. "Here it is!"

"Th-thank you." Marina hiccuped again.

"Now, blow," commanded Gerontissa. She waited.

Macrina blew her nose and dabbed at her eyes.

"Good," Gerontissa nodded. "Now, we go again."

Macrina was tall for her age, and Gerontissa was small and bent. They were almost the same height. Macrina's rubber boots squeaked a little as she walked. Gerontissa's robe rustled. Except for the birds in the trees and the faint sounds of the goats talking to each other in the animal farm behind her, Macrina heard nothing but quietness.

"Where is Sam?" she asked.

"Home," Gerontissa answered. "Home with Saucer and Sister Katherine and Sister Anna."

Macrina said nothing. She was glad Sam couldn't see her, but somehow she still felt awful.

"Now we stop," said Gerontissa.

Macrina looked up. The abbess was settling herself on a wooden bench beside the path, a few yards short of the church door. It was a wide, smooth bench, made from a big log that had been split in half and polished. One half of the log made the seat, and the other half made the back. Gerontissa laid her cane gently on the ground and patted the space next to her on the bench. Macrina sat down.

"Tell me," said Gerontissa.

Macrina hung her head, gripping the edge of the bench on either side of her. "I love the monastery," she began, her voice still squeaky with tears. "I come here every day in the summer, or at least I did. But when I came before, Sam wasn't here. I could work with the nuns or play in the garden. I could have prayers with you, and I could eat at the refectory. I even washed the dishes, and the sisters would say, 'Thank you, Macrina.' Sometimes I would lie in the grass and watch the tree leaves and the sky. This is my favorite place on earth."

Gerontissa patted her back. "And now?"

"Sam fights with me! Sam does everything wrong. He never follows the rules, and it bothers me so much. I fight with Sam because . . . I don't know why. I can't stop! This is from a mistake—I know it is! God wrecked everything for me because I didn't do what He liked." Macrina's voice broke, and she burst into tears again, her body drooping and shaking in the waves of a sorrow she could not control.

"Little one! Little one!" Gerontissa laid her arms gently around Macrina and cuddled her. The warm black habit brushed Macrina's face and soaked up her tears. The fragrance of incense drifted around her like a cloud. With a long, shuddering sigh, Macrina stopped crying and closed her eyes.

"Do you know what is the biggest rule we follow here?" whispered Gerontissa, stroking the straggling wisps of Macrina's hair back from her face.

"Sister Katherine wouldn't tell me," croaked Macrina. "She said to think about it, but the more I think, the more I don't know. I want to know the rule so I don't break it."

"Love is the rule," whispered Gerontissa, and her soft voice rustled like the breeze that rose suddenly around them, breaking the heated stillness of the afternoon.

"Love?"

"Love."

Reluctantly, Macrina sat up. "How can love be a rule? I can't follow it if I don't know. That must be why—"

Gerontissa put up her hand. "Let go of that," she said. "Rules are not what you think. You think the rule is in charge. The rule makes you do what you should do. No. This is not so."

Macrina stared at her. "No?"

"No." The abbess shook her head vigorously. "No, no."

Cool fingers of breeze caressed Macrina's face. Across the path, the blades of grass waved and danced in the sunlight. She blinked.

"What is a rule?" she asked, turning back to the abbess.

"It just describe." Gerontissa gestured with her hand. "How can I say . . . The rule is not the boss. God is the boss. The rule is how we make a picture of what God likes."

Macrina frowned. "Yes, and then we have to do what it describes, or He won't like it."

Gerontissa sighed. "Forgive me, little one. It is a big thing for these little words to carry."

For a few minutes, they were silent. Gerontissa's lips moved. Perhaps she was working out how to explain her thought. Perhaps she was praying.

"So." Gerontissa nodded. "I know. How do you feel, when you do what the rule says?"

"I feel good," Macrina answered promptly. "I like to follow the rules."

Gerontissa leaned closer. "You feel good and also what else?"

"What else?"

"Do you feel good only? Or is there another feeling?"

Macrina thought hard. "Relieved?"

"Yes! And do you know why?"

"Because I'm relieved I didn't make a mistake."

Gerontissa was smiling now. Her face wrinkled in a hundred places, and her eyes were full of light. "And what is so bad about making mistake?"

Macrina was startled. "Mistakes are bad!"

"Why?" crowed Gerontissa. "Why are they bad?"

Macrina paused and looked around. They were alone on the bench, alone in the world.

"Because of God," she whispered. "When I do good, God will make good things happen, but if I make a mistake, bad things will happen. God controls everything. So everything matters—all the mistakes." She shuddered.

"No, no, little one! This is why you don't know the rule! I prayed to know, and now I know."

"Oh, dear!" cried Macrina, wringing her hands. "It's another mistake!"

"Hush," said the abbess gently. "Now you listen. It is very simple." She took Macrina's sad face in her soft, wrinkled old hands and looked into her eyes. "You are not God, little one. God is God."

"I know, Gerontissa."

"No. You think, but you do not know. What you do does not control God. What you do does not control the world. Can you make it rain?"

"No, Gerontissa."

"Can you make Sam do what you want?"

"No."

"You do not control any of these things. You control only you. God is too big for you to control. You can never be God. Only God is big enough to be God."

Macrina sat very still, her face cradled in Gerontissa's hands.

"You were thinking like the old days, before Christ," explained Gerontissa. "You think if Moses speak to you and you say 'no,' the plagues will come for you."

Macrina's eyes popped, and her mouth fell open. How did Gerontissa know this? Macrina had told no one but her mother. How did Gerontissa know?

Gerontissa chuckled. "Yes, you think frogs and rivers of blood will come to you. I know. But we have Christ! Now, rules are different thing. Christ died on the cross for doing nothing wrong ever. Is this fair? Is this a good rule following?"

"No," answered Macrina, surprised. "It's not fair at all!"

"So, why does He do it?" Gerontissa gazed at her intently.

"For love?"

"Glory to God, little one! For love! It is for love!" Gerontissa laughed joyfully, and the breeze danced around them. The leaves of nearby trees rustled as if they clapped their hands. "That is all!" cried Gerontissa. "That is the rule that God follows. It is the only one we have."

CHAPTER 13

EARLY THE NEXT MORNING, Macrina stood at the monastery gate, waiting for Sam to arrive. She could see him coming, walking toward her down the dusty road, holding Saucer's leash. Saucer pranced beside him, sniffing the ground, sniffing Sam's shoes, and gazing up at Sam's face.

"Love is the only rule," Macrina reminded herself. "Love is the only rule. Love-is-the-only-rule-be-nice-to-Sam-breathe-through-your-nose-because-it-might-help-you-be-calm."

Sam reached the monastery gate and stopped

walking. Saucer sat down on his haunches, letting his tongue hang out of his mouth and wave like a flag.

Macrina and Sam eyed each other.

"Saucer is my dog," said Sam loudly. "He lives at my house now."

"That's very nice," Macrina said politely.

"You got stuck," continued Sam. "I went home because you got stuck."

"Stuck?" Macrina was stunned. "What do you mean, 'stuck'?"

"Stuck," repeated Sam. "It was interesting. People think I am the only one who gets stuck."

Macrina opened her mouth, but there were so many words in her head that she couldn't choose any to use.

"Stuck." Sam nodded at her.

"Are you being nice to me?" squeaked Macrina. "Is that what you think you're doing?"

Sam switched Saucer's leash to his left hand and hooked his right thumb through his belt loop. "I think so." He paused to consider. "Yes. I'm being nice."

Macrina's face turned red. "How is it nice to tell me I got stuck?!?"

"Because you *did* get stuck!"

"Well, I'm not stuck now!" Macrina turned her back and started walking. Sam watched her for a second then called out, "You know what I heard a nun say once?"

Macrina stopped midstride. She had to know. "What? What did a nun say once?"

"The truth will set you free. That's what she said."

"Yes, that's in the Bible."

"Sure is," agreed Sam. He unhooked his thumb, put Saucer's leash back in his right hand, and walked toward her. Macrina took a few deep breaths through her nose and waited for him.

"I bet you think it's pretty weird for me to tell you a Bible verse," Sam remarked.

"Why?" asked Macrina, suspiciously.

"You don't think I know any Bible verses," Sam replied.

"Oh." Macrina wanted to disagree with him, but she thought it might be dishonest. Did *anyone* think Sam knew Bible verses?

"I talked to my mom about you," Sam continued. "She said to talk things over and make peace."

"Thank you," said Macrina, uncertainly.

"Don't say 'thank you' yet. We aren't done."

"What do you mean?" Macrina stopped walking. Sam stopped walking. Saucer sat down on Sam's foot.

They had reached the bookstore. Probably the nuns were inside. This was already the longest conversation Macrina had ever had with Sam, and she had no idea what was coming next.

"You got stuck." Sam pointed toward the animal farm. "You were so mad you couldn't stop being mad."

Macrina's mouth fell open.

"I don't like that," said Sam in a low voice.

"What?" gasped Macrina. "What are you doing? Are you criticizing me?"

"I'm saying what happened," said Sam doggedly. "I'm saying you got stuck because you did get stuck. And I'm saying I didn't like it."

"Well, I don't like what you do! I don't like how you break rules and nobody cares!" Macrina threw her hands in the air. "I don't like how you told Sister Katherine I scrubbed the bunny hutch wrong! You know what else? I don't like that I had a horrible day yesterday! Do you think I was bawling my eyes out on the stepladder for fun?"

"You're doing it again," said Sam, taking a wary step back.

"No, I'm not!" shouted Macrina.

Saucer leaped up and started barking at Macrina.

Out of the corner of her eye, Macrina thought she saw a movement inside the bookstore window. Her face crumpled. "I'm doing it again!" she wailed. "I'm making mistakes again and again!"

Sam stopped backing away. "That's what I said."

"Why can't you be nice to me?" asked Macrina in a squeaky voice, swallowing the lump in her throat. "Why can't you ever just be *nice*?"

"I *AM* being nice!" roared Sam, losing his patience. "THE TRUTH WILL SET YOU FREE! I AM TELLING THE TRUTH!"

Macrina squeezed her hands tightly together and shut her eyes. "Love is the only rule, love is the only rule, love is the only rule," she murmured.

"STOP TALKING TO YOURSELF!" bellowed Sam. "TALK TO ME! THIS IS A CONVERSATION. YOU HAVE TO TALK TO ME!"

"LOVE IS THE ONLY RULE!" shouted Macrina.

Saucer barked at Macrina, then at Sam, and bounced in a circle around them, his eyes rolling from one to the other. The noise of his barking covered a small, scuffling sound behind them as Sister Katherine tried to step out of the bookstore and Sister Anna grabbed her arm and pulled her back in.

"TRUTH! TELL THE TRUTH! TRUTH TRUTH TRUTH!" trumpeted Sam.

Macrina threw back her head. "LOVE-LOVE-LOVE-LOVE!"

"TRUTH!"

"LOVE!"

Saucer stopped barking. He sat down on Sam's foot.

Macrina opened her eyes. "It's the same thing,

Sam," she said slowly. "We're saying the same thing."

"Truth will make you free," Sam repeated, still loud, but no longer roaring.

"Love is the only rule," Macrina answered.

In the open doorway behind them, Sister Anna let go of Sister Katherine's arm. "Now," she whispered. "Now you can tell them about the barn."

"Thank you," whispered Sister Katherine. "You're absolutely right."

CHAPTER 14

Sister Katherine and Sister Anna led Macrina, Sam, and Saucer to the animal farm. There was nothing surprising about that. They still needed to paint the bunny hutch, the henhouse, and Saucer's doghouse. Macrina saw that the hot sun had dried everything they had scrubbed. She was just opening her mouth to ask where the paint was when she realized that they were all still walking.

"Where are we going?" Macrina asked.

"To the barn!" Sister Katherine sounded excited.

"It's right there," said Sam. He pointed to the long,

low building beyond the little farm. It stood between the back fence and the woods, a few yards away from the building that housed the nuns and their guests. Saucer bounced on Sam's foot, and Sam stopped walking for a minute to take off Saucer's leash. He folded it carefully and crammed it into the pocket of his shorts. Saucer didn't need a leash at the monastery, but he would need one for the walk home at the end of the day. Sam rested his hand on his over-stuffed pocket, and his face relaxed.

Sister Anna was shorter than all of them except Saucer, but she reached the barn before anyone else. "Here's the scaffold!" she sang out.

Sure enough, there was a long, sturdy scaffold, about waist high, standing against the side of the barn. Cans of paint, clean brushes, some fat black pencils, and an icon were arranged on the scaffold platform.

"Are we going to paint the barn?" asked Macrina. "Didn't the families just paint it last fall?"

"Yes, they did," Sister Katherine smiled at her. "And they did a very nice job. Look at that beautiful clean red paint."

Macrina and Sam looked at the wall of the barn. Saucer plopped down next to Sam and looked at the barn too. It was obvious from his expression that he wondered what the people thought they were looking at.

"Can you guess what we want you to do?" asked Sister Anna.

"No guessing," said Sam firmly.

"Love even rude people," Macrina whispered to herself.

"We want you to paint some angels on this barn,"

said Sister Anna, clasping her hands together joyfully but keeping her voice calm. "Big angels. Angels as big as you, so we can all see them no matter where we are in the animal farm, no matter what we are doing."

"How will we draw them?" asked Macrina. These angels would be large and visible. She didn't want to make a mistake.

"Trace," said Sam, after a moment. "You get up there, and I'll trace around you. You can be the angel shape."

Macrina stared at him.

"We'll trace," Sam repeated, loudly. "Go stand on the scaffold like an angel."

"Here's an icon," said Sister Katherine, pointing to where she had set the Guardian Angel icon up against the frame on one end of the scaffold.

"Trace with paint?" squeaked Macrina.

Sam grinned. "Don't worry. I'll use these pencils. Look at them. Big ones. Those will make good marks."

Macrina smiled with relief. Saucer barked and ran in a circle.

"Here goes!" Macrina placed her hands on the platform and hoisted herself up. Sam scrambled after her. He lifted the icon and held it close to his face, noticing every detail.

"Just look at this." He turned the icon toward Macrina. "Be like the icon, and I'll trace around you."

Macrina nodded. "And then you can be like the icon, and I'll trace you to be another angel next to mine."

"And then Saucer!" shouted Sam.

"Saucer's a dog," began Macrina.

"Put wings on him!" shouted Sam.

Macrina looked slightly shocked, but she closed her mouth and stared at the icon in her hands. The angel was beautiful, tall and strong, with golden wings and a peaceful face. Macrina set down the icon, backed up against the barn wall, and held out her arms gracefully, as if she had wings. She closed her eyes and listened to the soft, bumpy squeak of Sam's pencil passing around her, leaving the shape of an angel on the wall of the barn.

When he was finished, Macrina opened her eyes and turned to look. "It worked!" she cried joyfully. "I can look at the icon and color it in. That was a good idea, Sam."

"Now Saucer," said Sam, handing her the pencil. "I'll hold him where we want him, and you trace."

It took a few minutes to get Saucer into position

on the platform. He was happy to go wherever Sam was, but he was also happy to sniff all the paints and lick all the brush handles. He wanted to see the icon, too. Saucer was used to seeing icons at church. He had a friendly feeling for icons.

"Can you make him sit?" asked Macrina.

"No, he has to stand so we can see his wings," said Sam. "I know. I can put his leash on, just for a minute."

Surprisingly, Saucer stood perfectly still for Sam when the leash came out. Sam sat down next to him, held the leash, and patted Saucer with his other hand. "Go quick," said Sam. "This won't last."

Macrina did her best. It wasn't a perfect job.

"I know his shape," said Sam. "I'll fix it when I paint it."

"Now it's your turn," said Macrina.

Sam let Saucer off the leash and helped him off the platform. Saucer sat on his haunches, watching Sam.

"He always watches you," Macrina noticed.

"He knows he's my dog," said Sam.

Sam stood up on the platform, placing himself against the wall beside the tracing of Saucer. The tracing of Macrina was on the other side, so when they were finished, there would be two angels on the barn wall with a little dog angel between them.

"Now trace," said Sam. He did not close his eyes. He tried to watch Macrina's hand.

"Stop watching my hand," said Macrina. "It makes you wiggle too much."

"Stop bossing me," said Sam. "That makes me wiggle too much."

"Love is the only rule," Macrina repeated to herself.

"I can hear you when you talk to yourself," Sam told her, watching her trace his right arm.

"Well, then at least you know I am trying," said Macrina, gripping her pencil.

"Other people try hard too, not just you."

Macrina looked up. "I know that, Sam."

Sam did his best to hold still, and as the pencil moved up his arm and began to trace around his head, Sam saw that Macrina was smiling.

EPILOGUE

ON THE FIRST SUNDAY In September, Elias, Matthew, and Grace came back to church at the monastery. Elias and Matthew were sunburnt, and their hair had bleached to a pale gold color. Grace had her hair in cornrows, and the beads clinked softly as she turned to look around the familiar room. Her eyes went from icon to icon, from friend to friend, and her fingers cuddled a small flat rock inside her pocket, picked up from the monastery path that morning as she walked from the parking lot to the church.

Summer was over. Their families had traveled, and there would be many adventures to talk over after Liturgy.

For now, it was good to be home again, standing where they always stood on the clean wooden floor of the little stone church, singing the same hymns, praying the same prayers, smelling the sweet medley of incense and beeswax and the occasional whiffs of good cooking drifting over from the refectory. Everything was just the same as it had been when they went away. Nothing had changed.

Nothing?

Grace was the first to notice. She took a quick step sideways and grabbed Elias's arm. Her mama frowned and shook her head. Grace let go of Elias, but she stared at him very hard and rolled her eyes toward the back of the church.

Elias let his eyes wander, seeing the familiar faces around him. And then, he saw something that was not familiar at all.

He nudged his brother Matthew urgently with his elbow.

"Ow!" hissed Matthew. "What on earth?"

Elias rolled his eyes hard to the right and pointed with his chin. Matthew looked where he was pointing.

"Whoa," croaked Matthew, so surprised he forgot to be quiet.

"Shhh," whispered their mother.

Matthew looked at Elias. Elias nodded. They both mouthed the word "Whoa" to each other. Elias turned his head back to Grace, who stared at him and wiggled her eyebrows. Elias nodded. All three of them knew what they were talking about. Something this amazing could be said without words.

In the back of the church, Saucer sat peacefully on

his little square of green carpet. His bright eyes roamed the church but always came back to Sam. His pointed ears stood straight up, and his breath came in little puffs here in the warm, scented air. Sam stood to the left of the little corgi, moving his fingers along a prayer rope, counting and praying his way through church. And Macrina stood to the right of Saucer, sharing the square of carpet at the back of the church.

When the service ended, Sam would open the doors of the church as he always did, and Saucer would scamper out. One by one, their families and friends would come through those doors. Outside, the monastery path would be waiting, beginning at the church and winding along to every building and every garden, to the gate of the monastery and the smaller, squeaky gate of the animal farm. And anyone who cared to follow the path all the way to that small gate would see something wonderful beyond it on the wall of the barn, something they might have seen at the back of the church if God had opened their eyes.

They would see two beautiful angels, and a little brown dog with wings.

THE END

MELINDA JOHNSON is an Ortho-
dox Christian, wife, mother, and writer. She is the bemused and enchanted
guardian of a corgi named Ferdinand
who supervised the writing of this
book. Ferdinand also bosses Melinda's office, the deer in her backyard,
her family's daily schedule, and her
attempts to read quietly on the sofa. If
you enjoy this book, you may give all
the credit to Ferdinand.

LIVING ON A REAL FARM

Because Sam and Saucer, and Macrina and the nuns at the Monastery of St. Gerasim are fictional, we wanted to ask a real Orthodox Christian farm family to tell us a little bit about life today on a farm. Enjoy this short piece by Veronica—relating what it's like living side by side with a whole barn full of animals.

I HAVE TWO MILK COWS and a beef steer. I also have eleven sheep including three lambs and more ducks than I can count; so many ducks! In the summers, I keep turkeys and pigs. One of my favorite times of the year is the lambing season when there are many baby lambs ready to be snuggled.

In the mornings, I have to get up early to help milk the cows, even if I don't feel like it. Sometimes when I am walking out to the barn, I am tired and grumpy, but as soon as I get out to the barn, I see the sheep there, staring at me, waiting to be let out. It makes me happy to see their cheerful, furry faces. In the middle of the day, I have to make sure that all the animals have water and I also have to make sure that none of the lambs have gotten lost. They might not realize that they are lost while they are wandering away. I go out and count all the lambs to make sure they are all there.

We put the animals in the barn at night to protect them from predators like coyotes and owls. The cattle don't need to be put in because they have chased off coyotes with their horns. They are very sweet to people, but they don't like predators. I give them hay and grain and water, and sometimes I pick up the lambs, even when they are getting so big that I can barely hold them. They are so used to being snuggled that they rub their faces in my hair.

Not all of my animals live in the barn. I also have a show rabbit, and one of my sisters has one, too. They live in the house in the room that used to be the farm office, but now the office is upstairs. My rabbit likes to run around the living room, ripping pages out of books, and jumping into people's laps because he thinks it is a game. Lightening is so sweet, but he does not realize that he is not supposed to rip pages out of books.

Since my dad is a priest, he blesses the animals every year at Mid-Pentecost. Once, Bishop John of Caracas and South America was visiting the monastery here. He came to dinner because he wanted to bless the animals himself. My mom made a nice dinner and put out her best tablecloth, but he decided that he wanted to eat outside and feed the turkeys from his plate. A long time ago, he was the first monk here. He would use a snowmobile to go out into the woods and see the wolves. They never hurt him. Everything loves him, it doesn't matter if they are people or animals. Even the wolves love him.

Even though my animals are a lot of work, they are also a lot of fun. I like living on a farm because it means that I can play with cows and snuggle with lambs whenever I feel like it. I have learned to work very hard because if I don't, I won't be able to have cows, sheep, poultry, rabbits, and pigs. I like teaching other people about where their food comes from. I have learned many lessons that are important, such as the proper way to lead a cow around so they won't step on your feet, how to halter break an animal, and how to take care of a pregnant ewe. I hope that I will always have animals to care for and to snuggle.

Veronica and Princess

Veronica Naasko lives on a farm in the snowy north woods and raises beef and ducks and sheep. She is active in 4H and the county fair and is an aspiring writer with many idea notebooks. She is the daughter of an Orthodox priest and has five sisters and five brothers. This is her first published piece.

OTHER BOOKS IN THE SAM AND SAUCER SERIES

Shepherding Sam

Sam's Aunt Eva says he's like a tornado—he causes a ruckus everywhere he goes. But Aunt Eva won't give up on Sam, and neither will Saucer, the monastery's corgi puppy. Saucer lives at the monastery, but he dreams of herding sheep. With no sheep in his life, Saucer tries to herd everyone else—farm animals, nuns, and especially Sam. Sam doesn't want to follow anyone, not even a funny puppy. But Saucer knows that if he just keeps trying, he can bring this lonely boy back to the flock.
• ISBN: 9781944967079

The Barn and the Book

Sam wants to know if animals (especially Saucer!) can speak at midnight on Christmas Eve. Grace and Macrina are competing to write a story, and Elias is losing his patience. Meanwhile, Sister Anna hopes God will rescue her from teaching Sunday school. Christmas is coming, but hearts are full of secrets and frustrations. *The Barn and the Book* is a story about the traps we build when we try to see in the dark. We tumble into trouble and confusion on our own, but God can steer us clear of our traps and shine His kindly light into our darkness.
• ISBN: 9781944967437

Two-Book Bundle
Shepherding Sam & The Barn and the Book
• SKU 006015

OTHER BOOKS OF INTEREST

Spyridon's Shoes
by Christine Rogers

Young Spyros spends his days fishing, octopus hunting, and dreaming of attending school like his best friend, Niko. When he encounters an elderly man on the beach after an accident, his whole life begins to shift and change. But who is this mysterious, saintly man, and why is his friendship so important? Take a short trip back in time to the Greek island of Corfu and discover the real reason for the mystery surrounding Spyridon's shoes.
• Ages 7 to 12, Paperback, 104 pages,
ISBN: 9781944967468

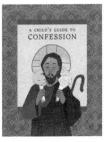

A Child's Guide to Confession
compiled and edited by Ancient Faith Publishing
illustrated by Nicholas Malara

An engaging, illustrated guide to confession for children. This 104-page, easy-to-use aid will help a child understand and prepare for confession. Designed for both younger and older children, this book assists the child with brief, inspirational thoughts followed by prayers and an age-appropriate self-examination based on 1 Corinthians 13 (the "love chapter"). *A Child's Guide to Confession* also includes a glossary of basic vocabulary that children typically encounter when learning about or going to confession. Fully illustrated in a simple, colorful, yet reverent style.
• Ages 5 to 12, Paperback, 104 pages, ISBN: 9781944967451

To purchase these books and others of interest, please visit our website:
store.ancientfaith.com

Ancient Faith Publishing hopes you have enjoyed and bene-fited from this book. The proceeds from the sales of our books only partially cover the costs of operating our nonprofit minis-try—which includes both the work of **Ancient Faith Publishing** and the work of **Ancient Faith Radio**. Your financial support makes it possible to continue this ministry both in print and online. Donations are tax-deductible and can be made at **www.ancientfaith.com.**

To view our other publications,
please visit our website: **store.ancientfaith.com**

 ANCIENT FAITH RADIO

Bringing you Orthodox Christian music, readings, prayers, teaching, and podcasts 24 hours a day since 2004 at
www.ancientfaith.com